Withdrawn

The Boxcar Children Mysteries

THE GREAT TURKEY HEIST

created by
GERTRUDE CHANDLER WARNER

Illustrated by Robert Papp

,

ALBERT WHITMAN & Company
Chicago, Illinois

Library of Congress Cataloging-in-Publication Data

Warner, Gertrude Chandler, 1890-1979.
The great turkey heist / by Gertrude Chandler Warner
illustrated by Robert Papp.
p.cm.
Summary: The four Alden children, aged six to fourteen, uncover
a mystery while volunteering at a food pantry for the needy.
ISBN: 978-0-8075-3050-4 (hardcover)
ISBN: 978-0-8075-3051-1 (paperback)
[1. Mystery and detective stories. 2. Generosity—Fiction.
3. Brothers and sisters—Fiction. 4. Orphans—Fiction.]
I. Papp, Robert, ill. II. Title.
PZ7.W244Gqi 2011   [Fic]—dc22

10 9 8 7 6 5 4 3 2 1 LB 16 15 14 13 12 11

Cover art by Robert Papp.

For information about Albert Whitman & Company,
visit our web site at www.albertwhitman.com.

Contents

THE GREAT TURKEY HEIST

CHAPTER 1

Aldens to the Rescue

"Watch this!" Six-year-old Benny Alden ran across the lawn at Grandfather's house and leaped into the huge pile of leaves under the maple tree.

Henry leaned on his rake and laughed. "That was your best jump yet," he said. But when Benny didn't pop up immediately, Henry got a little worried. "Benny? Are you okay?"

"Where did he go?" asked ten-year-old Violet. She was sweeping leaves off the path.

Watch, the Alden's wire terrier, barked anxiously. He dug into the pile of leaves, his tail wagging, until he found Benny hiding at the bottom.

"That was cool!" Benny said, jumping up and patting Watch on the head. "The pile is so big now that I can hide in it! I'm going to make a tunnel." Benny burrowed beneath the dried leaves with Watch close behind.

Violet looked up at the trees. She caught a red maple leaf that floated down on the cool breeze. "What a pretty color," she said. "There are still so many more leaves to fall. We have a lot more work to do."

Just then, Jessie came out on the porch. "It's almost time to go," she called to her sister and brothers. "We should start to clean up. We told Grandfather that we would meet him at 12:30."

Benny hopped up from the pile and threw a fistful of leaves into the air. "But where are we going?" he asked.

"It's not like you to forget a lunch date, Benny!" Jessie said. "We are meeting

Grandfather at Green Fields, the new restaurant that just opened in town. The owner of Green Fields is one of Grandfather's friends."

"Oh right! I almost forgot, but my stomach sure didn't! Listen." Benny's stomach began to growl loudly. "I'm starved!"

"We'd better hurry, then." Henry laughed. "We don't want to keep Benny's stomach waiting. It sounds dangerous!" Benny was famous for his big appetite and growling stomach. "I'll dump these leaves back in the woods," Henry said. At fourteen, Henry was the oldest of the four Alden children.

"I'll help you, Henry," said Violet.

Jessie began to brush the leaves from Benny's jacket and to smooth out his hair. "Can't have you looking messy for our lunch date," she teased. Jessie was twelve and often acted like a mother to her younger brother.

The Aldens were orphans. After their parents died, they ran away and lived on their own in an old abandoned boxcar in the woods. Their grandfather found them and brought them to live with him in his big house in Greenfield.

The Aldens hopped on their bicycles and headed into town. Henry led the way. They stopped at the corner of Chestnut and Main Streets to wait for the light to turn green. A man in a blue shirt was crossing Main Street. He was struggling with a large box that appeared to be very heavy. Just then, another man wearing a dark brown hat and scarf hurried into the street. He shoved the man with the box as he walked past.

"Oh my!" Violet cried.

The man in the blue shirt tumbled to the ground. The box he was carrying broke open, and canned goods rolled every which way. The light turned green, but the cars could not move. There were cans all over the street! Impatient drivers began to honk their horns.

"Out of my way!" cried the man in a hurry. He pulled his brown hat low and quickly walked away.

"How rude!" Jessie exclaimed.

The Aldens jumped from their bicycles. Henry helped the man to his feet. Jessie and Henry quickly picked up the cans in the street. Violet and Benny collected those that had rolled to the sidewalk.

"Are you all right, sir?" asked Violet.

The man was brushing off his pants. "Yes, thank you, I will be fine. I'm not even sure what happened."

Henry placed the last of the cans in the pile on the sidewalk. "Someone bumped you from behind. He seemed to be in quite a hurry."

Jessie looked down the street to where the man had disappeared. "It almost looked like he did it on purpose. Did you know him?"

"I didn't really see him," said the man in the blue shirt. "Everything happened so fast. What did he look like?"

"He was wearing a dark brown scarf and hat," said Violet. "I couldn't see his face. Maybe he just wasn't paying attention to where he was going."

"You're probably right. Thank you for all your help," said the man. "My name is Brian

Grayson. It's nice to meet you."

Jessie introduced the Aldens. "I'm afraid your box is broken, Mr. Grayson," she said.

Mr. Grayson sighed. "Yes, I see." He tried to pick up the cans, but there were too many for him to carry.

"We have baskets on our bicycles," Henry said. "We could put the cans in there and deliver them for you to wherever you are going."

"Yes," Jessie said. "We would be happy to do that. We are meeting our grandfather for lunch, but I am sure he will understand if we are a few minutes late."

"Where are you having lunch?" asked Mr. Grayson.

"At Green Fields restaurant," Violet said. "It's new."

"And I'm starved!" Benny added.

Mr. Grayson smiled widely. "What a coincidence! Green Fields restaurant is just where I am going."

"Have you ever eaten there before?" asked Benny, placing cans of corn into his basket.

"Oh yes," said Mr. Grayson. "Many times."

"Is the food good?" Benny asked.

"Well, I sure think so. But I'm prejudiced." Mr. Grayson winked at the Aldens.

With their baskets filled with canned goods, the children pedaled slowly behind Mr. Grayson toward Green Fields. Grandfather was standing in front of the restaurant. He was checking his watch.

When he looked up, Grandfather smiled at the group approaching him.

"Well, Brian, it looks like you have already met my grandchildren!" Grandfather said.

"I have, James," Mr. Grayson said, shaking Grandfather's hand. "They came to my rescue a few minutes ago."

Grandfather looked puzzled.

"I'll explain inside," Mr. Grayson said. "Why don't you leave your bicycles here, children? I will have my employees come out and collect the cans from your baskets."

"Your employees?" asked Henry.

"Yes," said Mr. Grayson. "Green Fields is my restaurant." He held the door open for the Aldens. "Come on in and let me show it to you."

"How beautiful!" Violet exclaimed once they all got inside.

Tables and booths were arranged on a grass-green carpet. The sky-blue ceiling was decorated with fluffy painted clouds. Plants hung near every table and grew in containers in the corners as well. A waterfall trickled into a fountain in the center of the room. Even the chairs had green leaves painted on their sides.

"And it smells good, too!" Benny said.

Mr. Grayson smiled. "I'm so glad you like it." He led the Aldens to a big table. "Make yourselves comfortable," he said.

A young waitress approached the table. "Hello, Noreen," said Mr. Grayson. "These are the Aldens, and they are my special guests for lunch today."

"Hello," said Noreen. "Welcome to Green Fields. Would anyone like a glass of fresh apple cider?"

"Yes, please," answered Jessie. "We all love apple cider."

"I'll bring it right over for you, along with some of our wheat rolls," said Noreen. "They just came out of the oven!"

Mr. Grayson sat with the Aldens.

"I like your restaurant," said Benny. "It looks really cool in here. And I'll bet the food is good, too!"

"Thank you," said Mr. Grayson. "Everything we serve here is organic."

Benny looked puzzled. "What is that?" he asked.

"It means that all the food we serve is grown or raised naturally, without chemicals. We buy most of our food from local farmers," Mr. Grayson explained.

"But then why did you have all those cans?" Benny asked. "They don't come from a farm, do they?"

Mr. Grayson laughed. "No. They don't come from a farm. They are donations that I was collecting."

Benny gazed around the cozy restaurant. "You take donations for your restaurant?"

Mr. Grayson shook his head. "It's not

for the restaurant, Benny. It's for the food pantry."

Benny was very confused. "Food . . . what?"

Jessie smiled. "Food pantry. It is a place where people who don't have a lot of money can get groceries for free for their families."

"I didn't know we had a food pantry in Greenfield," Grandfather said. "I've never seen it."

"It's a new idea of mine," Mr. Grayson said. "I started the food pantry about a month ago. First, I rented a store. I tried to fix it up inside. Then I put lots of shelves in for the food."

"That's a wonderful idea," said Grandfather.

"I'm afraid it hasn't been going too well," Mr. Grayson said. "I don't have enough food to put on the shelves. And almost no one knows that we even have a food pantry in Greenfield."

"It must be hard to start a new restaurant and a food pantry at the same time," Henry said.

"You're right, Henry. But when I was growing up, my family didn't have much money. Sometimes we didn't have enough food to eat. I remember going to bed very hungry on many nights. I want to have a nice restaurant, but I also want to make sure that no one in our town has to go to bed hungry. But I guess I just don't have enough time to do everything."

Benny looked sad. "I'm always hungry," he said. "But Mrs. McGregor makes great meals for me. It would be awful to be hungry and not have a dinner to eat. My stomach would hurt a lot." Mrs. McGregor was the Aldens' housekeeper and a wonderful cook, as well.

"We could help you with the food pantry, Mr. Grayson," said Violet.

"Yes," said Jessie. "We would love to help out."

"Are you sure?" asked Mr. Grayson. "I've only just begun to set it up. It will take a lot of hard work."

Grandfather smiled. "My grandchildren don't mind hard work," he said. "And they are very helpful."

"That would be wonderful!" said Mr.

Grayson. "James, your grandchildren have rescued me twice today." Mr. Grayson explained about the fall he took in the street and the mysterious man in the dark brown hat and scarf who had hurried away.

"That's very odd," said Grandfather. "Thank goodness you weren't hurt."

Mr. Grayson gave Henry the address of the food pantry. "If you four can meet me there tomorrow morning, I can show you what needs to be done."

Just then, a tall woman walked into the restaurant. She banged a can of green beans onto the table right in front of Mr. Grayson. "I found this on the street, Brian," she said. "I saw you spill those canned goods. You should stop lying to people about the food you serve here."

Some customers looked up to see what was happening. Mr. Grayson stood. "Betty, I never lie to my customers. Please leave this restaurant."

"I'll leave," the tall woman said. "But this restaurant is a fraud!"

Mr. Grayson sat back down. "I'm so sorry," he said to the Aldens. "That was Betty Matthews. She owns Harvest Restaurant. I don't think she likes that I have opened my restaurant right across the street from her."

Benny looked out the window. He watched Betty Matthews march back into Harvest Restaurant.

Just then, Noreen approached the table with glasses of apple cider, wheat rolls, and a huge tray of food. "I thought you might like to sample all of our most popular dishes," she said, placing the tray on the center of the table. "Mr. Grayson said you were special guests!"

"Oh boy!" Benny exclaimed. "Pass me everything!"

Jessie looked at her little brother.

"Excuse me," Benny said. "Pass me everything, please."

Everyone laughed and filled their plates with the delicious food. They quickly forgot about Betty Matthews and her rude outburst.

CHAPTER 2

A Mysterious Crash

At the breakfast table, Benny excitedly told Mrs. McGregor about all the good food at the Green Fields restaurant.

"I hope all that good food didn't fill you up too much," Mrs. McGregor said as she set a plate of apple-cinnamon pancakes in front of Benny.

Benny couldn't answer. His mouth was already full of the warm, tasty breakfast.

Henry laughed. "It's impossible to fill Benny up too much," he said.

Benny swallowed. "These pancakes are so good! You should open up a restaurant, Mrs. McGregor. Nobody can cook better than you can!"

Mrs. McGregor beamed. "Thank you, Benny. But why are you children eating so quickly? There are plenty more pancakes."

Jessie explained that they had agreed to help out at the new food pantry this morning.

Benny put down his fork for a moment. "Some people don't have enough to eat, Mrs. McGregor. I wish I could share these pancakes with them."

"That's very kind of you, Benny," Mrs. McGregor said. "But you should eat a good breakfast. You will need lots of energy if you are going to work hard at the food pantry." Mrs. McGregor set another platter of pancakes on the table. "I would like to help, too. I can make some cakes and pies. Do you think they would accept them at the food pantry?"

"Oh yes," Violet answered. "I'm sure they would love them."

After the children cleaned up the breakfast table, they jumped on their bicycles and headed toward the address that Mr. Grayson had given to Henry.

"It has to be somewhere around here," Henry said, stopping his bike and staring at the written address. "But I don't see it."

The children looked at all the addresses on Chestnut Street. There was a grocery store, a dress shop, a movie theater, and a hardware store. But they did not see a food pantry.

Suddenly, Jessie looked up and noticed that Benny was missing.

"Benny! Benny!" she called. "Where are you?"

"I'm over here, Jessie."

Jessie still did not see her little brother. She ran toward his voice.

Benny popped out of a very small alley. "I think I found the food pantry," he said.

Jessie, Henry, and Violet followed Benny down the dark alley.

"I never knew this alley was here," said Henry.

"It's very dark," said Violet. "I don't like it. How did you ever find this, Benny?"

Benny pointed to a corner. "I saw that cat come in here and I followed it." A yellow cat was curled on top of an old trash can.

"Look there!" Jessie said. There was a gray door at the end of the alley. Someone had taped a sign to the door. It read, "Greenfield Food Pantry."

"How did you know this was the food pantry, Benny?" asked Henry. "Were you able to read the sign?"

Benny was just learning how to read. "I thought it said *food*, but I wasn't sure," Benny said. "Then I found a clue that helped me." Benny showed Henry a small bin by the door. It had several cans of corn and beans in it.

"Good detective work, Benny!" said Jessie.

Suddenly the door flew open, and the children jumped back in surprise. Mr. Grayson had an angry look on his face. When he saw the Aldens, he relaxed.

"I'm sorry to startle you, children," Mr.

Grayson said. He rubbed his hands through his hair. "It's just that someone has been playing tricks on me. The sign I made was stolen from my door this morning. I had to tape up this paper sign in its place. I thought maybe you were the thieves coming back."

"How terrible!" Jessie said. "Who would do such a thing?"

"I don't know." Mr. Grayson looked very tired. "But come on in, kids. I'll show you around."

"This is a food pantry?" asked Benny, looking around the dim building.

"Yes, but not a very good one, I'm afraid," Mr. Grayson said.

Boxes were scattered around the mostly-empty-building. Metal shelves were set up in aisles, but they were dusty. A few cans and boxes of cereal sat on the shelves. The floor was dirty. A lightbulb in the corner flickered on and off.

"There are some donations in those boxes," Mr. Grayson said. "But I haven't decided on the best place to put them yet."

Jessie's arms were folded. She looked up and down the entire room. "Mr. Grayson," she said, "I think the first thing we need to do is clean up. If you have a mop and a bucket, I can start by washing the floors."

"Benny and I can dust those shelves," Violet offered.

"Is there a ladder in the back?" Henry asked. "I will change the lightbulbs and make it brighter in here."

Mr. Grayson nodded. "Your grandfather was right. You children are helpful!"

Mr. Grayson showed the children the back room. It had plenty of cleaning supplies. Soon, he needed to leave for the restaurant. "Are you sure that you will be okay here by yourselves?" he asked.

"We'll be fine," Jessie answered. She had already filled her bucket with hot, soapy water.

Once Mr. Grayson left, Violet and Benny used rags and a bottle of spray to shine up all the shelves.

Henry found a box of lightbulbs. He set up

the ladder and began to remove the old ones.

"This place sure is a mess," Jessie said, wringing out her mop.

"Yes," Violet agreed. She wiped a cobweb from the corner of a shelf. "But even after it is clean, I am afraid it will still look dreary. It is not a very pleasant place for a food pantry."

Henry stood on top of the ladder. "Violet is right," he said. "Now that the room is brighter, I can see how bad things are."

Benny pointed. "Look," he said. "There are even some holes in the walls."

"I can fix those," Henry said.

"And maybe we can paint the walls a more cheerful color," Jessie added.

The children were standing together near the ladder when they heard a loud crash at the door. Everyone jumped.

"What was that?" Benny asked.

Violet took Benny's hand.

"Stay there," Jessie said to her sister and brother. "Henry and I will check it out."

There were no windows to look outside into the alley. Henry slowly opened the door. Something red dripped down the door. Garbage was scattered in the alley.

"What's that smell?" Benny held his hand over his nose. "It's terrible."

Henry opened the door wide. "It looks like a trash can full of garbage was overturned."

Jessie looked up the alley. There was no one there. The small yellow cat picked through the mess.

"Do you think the cat knocked over the trash can?" asked Violet.

"No," Henry said. "Someone threw the trash can against our door." He looked up at the red-liquid stain on the top of the door. A ketchup bottle lay broken beneath it on the ground. "For one thing, the cat could not get to the garbage up that high. And also, the sign that Mr. Grayson taped to the door is gone. I'll be right back."

Henry jumped over a half-eaten sandwich and an empty soda bottle. He ran up the alley to Chestnut Street. He looked up and down the street. He only saw shoppers and people out for a stroll. No one looked suspicious.

Jessie swept the garbage into a pile. Violet helped to dump it all back into the trash can. When they were done cleaning up, the children went back inside. They sat in a circle on the floor.

"I don't see how this food pantry will ever work," Jessie said.

"There's not much food here," Benny said. "It is not enough to fill up very many people."

Henry looked toward the door. "And someone is trying hard to hurt this food pantry."

Jessie looked at her brother. "Do you think that the person who threw the garbage could be the same person who knocked Mr. Grayson to the ground?"

"It could be," Henry said.

"But why would anyone not like a food pantry?" asked Benny.

Henry shook his head. "I don't understand it, either," he said. "It doesn't make any sense."

Violet had been sitting very quietly. Now she suddenly stood up. "The person who did this is not going to stop the food pantry," she said. "We are going to make it a big success. If Mr. Grayson agrees, we will paint the walls and the door outside, too. I can paint the name of the food pantry right on the door. No one will be able to steal it then."

"But there's no food," Benny said. His stomach was already growling for lunch.

"A new sign is a good idea, Violet," Jessie said. "But Benny is right. It will not help if there is no food on the shelves."

Violet looked thoughtful. "Maybe it will," she said. "I have an idea."

Just then, there was a faint scratching at the door. The children sat very still.

"Do you think the bad person is back?" whispered Benny.

The scratching noise continued.

Jessie opened the door a crack. She peeked outside. She felt something brush against her legs and she jumped back. It was the yellow cat! It snuck into the room and sat right next to Benny. It mewed.

The children laughed.

"This time it *was* the cat!" Benny said.

Violet found a bowl and a small can of tuna fish in the cupboard in the back room. She set it out for the cat.

"Poor little thing," she said. "You must be very hungry."

The cat began to quickly eat the tuna fish. Violet ran her fingers through the cat's soft fur. "This cat is our first customer at the food pantry!" she said.

"I suppose you are right about that, Violet," Henry said. "I hope she is not our last."

Benny's stomach growled so loudly that even the cat looked up.

"Sorry," Benny said. "I guess all this talk of food is making my stomach go crazy."

Henry laughed. "The cat is not the only hungry one in this room. Let's go get some lunch, and Violet can tell us about her ideas."

CHAPTER 3

Mind Your Own Business!

Henry, Jessie, Violet, and Benny sat in a back booth at Green Fields restaurant. Jessie squirted ketchup on Benny's burger.

Noreen, the waitress, set four cold glasses of apple cider on the table. "Mr. Grayson is a little busy in the kitchen right now," she said. "But he'll be out to talk with you as soon as he can."

"Of course," Jessie said. "We understand."

Violet took a long drink of her cider. "I was thinking," she said, "that we need a lot of donations if we are going to fill up the shelves at the food pantry. I will paint a sign on the door. But no one will see it. We need to let everyone know about the food pantry."

"How about flyers?" Jessie asked.

Violet took a bite of her salad. "Yes," she said. "We could make flyers and put them up around town."

"The grocery store would be the best place," Henry said.

Jessie agreed. "People could buy food and donate it right at the checkout!"

"And we could set up donation jars, too," Violet said.

Benny took a gulp of his apple cider. "What's a donation jar?" he asked.

Violet reached for a large glass container of mustard. She put it in the center of the table. "We could clean out jars like this, Benny," she said. "Then we could tape a small sign to the front asking for donations. If stores will put them on their checkout counters, people could drop their change into the jar. We could use that money to buy more food for the food pantry."

Mr. Grayson walked up to the booth. He was wearing a white apron and carrying a warm apple pie. "May I join you for some dessert?" he asked.

"Oh boy!" Benny said. "Pie!"

Noreen brought five plates and five forks and sliced the pie. Everyone had a large piece.

"Mr. Grayson," Henry said. "We were wondering if we could paint the food pantry."

"It's clean now," Jessie added. "But it is still dark inside. Maybe a fresh coat of paint would brighten it up."

"That sounds wonderful!" Mr. Grayson said.

"And Violet can paint a sign on the door," Benny mumbled, his mouth full of pie. "Violet is a good artist. She can draw anything!"

Violet's face turned red. "Not anything, Benny," she said. "But I'm sure I can design a nice sign for your door, Mr. Grayson."

"And no one better throw garbage on it!" Benny said as he ate the last crumb from his plate.

Mr. Grayson looked confused. "Garbage?"

Henry explained what had happened earlier at the food pantry.

Mr. Grayson seemed surprised. "You weren't hurt, were you?" he asked.

"Oh no," Jessie said. "Nothing like that. It was just messy."

Mr. Grayson crossed his arms. He stared out the window. "I don't understand it," he said. "Who could be doing these things?"

Noreen hurried up to the table. "I'm sorry to interrupt," she said. "You are needed in the kitchen, Mr. Grayson."

"Sorry, children," he said. "I have a lot of work to do. But if you want to paint the food pantry, you can get the supplies at the hardware store. I will call Mr. Carroll. He will put the charges on my account." Mr. Grayson got up and walked back to the kitchen.

"Mr. Grayson sure is a busy man," Benny said.

"Yes," said Violet. "And he seems quite upset about the problems with the food pantry."

"We should get to the hardware store," Henry said. "We have a lot of work to do."

The children parked their bicycles in the alley by the food pantry. They walked around the corner to the hardware store. Inside, they looked at all the color choices for paint.

"There must be every color in the rainbow here," Jessie said. "How will we ever choose?"

Violet admired all the many shades of purple. It was her favorite color.

"This one matches your hair ribbons and your shoelaces," Benny said, pointing to a pretty shade of violet.

Violet smiled. She often wore something purple with each of her outfits. "Yes, it does, Benny. And look! This color matches your shirt." Violet showed her brother a golden-yellow paint.

"That yellow would certainly brighten up the food pantry," Jessie said.

"I agree," Henry added.

"Can I help you kids?" A dark-haired man in a flannel shirt stood in the aisle. "I'm Mr. Carroll. Are you the Aldens?" he asked.

"Yes," Jessie answered. She introduced her sister and brothers. "We're here for some paint."

"Mr. Grayson told me you would be stopping by. Did you pick out a color?"

"We think this golden-yellow would brighten up the walls," Jessie said.

"That's a good choice," Mr. Carroll agreed. "I'll get you started with a few cans. If you run low, you can come back for more."

Mr. Carroll grabbed a cart. He mixed the paint. Then he put the cans in the cart. He also put brushes, rollers, and paint trays in the cart.

"Wow!" Benny said. "That's a lot of stuff. I can't wait to paint! I'm going to paint one whole wall by myself!"

Mr. Carroll laughed. "You might need your brother to help you with the high places," he said. "But if you are going to be painting, I think you need one more thing." Mr. Carroll pulled a box down from a shelf.

"What's that?" Benny asked.

"These are painter's overalls," he said.

"I think I have some small sizes in here. Here, try these on, Benny."

Benny slipped into the overalls. They were a little too long. Jessie rolled up the pant legs for him.

"Look at me!" Benny cried. "These even have a pocket in the front. I can put my brush in there!" Benny grabbed a brush from the cart and stuck it in the pocket. Everyone laughed.

"There's a pair for each of you here," Mr. Carroll said. "Help yourselves."

"Thank you," Henry said. "But we don't want to run Mr. Grayson's bill up too high. We should just get the paint and the brushes. We'll be careful not to get paint on our clothes."

"I insist," Mr. Carroll said. "I am donating all this to the food pantry."

"That is so kind. Thank you," Jessie said.

Mr. Carroll patted his round stomach. "I sure like to eat," he said. "I don't like to think of anyone being hungry. This is my way of helping. I will stop by later to see how you are making out."

The children thanked Mr. Carroll and carried their supplies back to the food pantry. The little yellow cat was waiting for them.

"Can we let the cat in again?" Benny asked.

"Sure," Jessie said. "She certainly seems to like you."

The cat rubbed itself against Benny's legs.

"Come on, Sunny. Come on," Benny said. He picked the cat up and held her in his arms.

"How do you know her name is Sunny?" asked Violet.

"That's easy!" Benny said. "She is yellow and she feels warm!"

Everyone laughed. Soon, they were all hard at work. Henry fixed the holes in the wall with material he found at the hardware store. Jessie took the wooden sticks Mr. Carroll had put in her bag and stirred the paint in the cans. She laid a blue tarp on the floor in the corner. Violet started outside, putting a nice, bright coat of paint on the door.

"You can start here, Benny," she said. "And I will start at the other end of this wall."

"Okay," Benny said. "And then we'll meet

in the middle!"

When Violet was done with the first coat on the door, she came inside. She took a small brush and started to paint on an empty wall. "How does this look?" she asked.

"Violet! That's wonderful," Jessie said.

Violet had painted *Greenfield Food Pantry* on the wall. Beneath it, she had painted a bright bowl overflowing with fruits and vegetables.

"But I thought you were going to paint it on the door," Benny said. "And all the fruits and vegetables are yellow."

Violet laughed. "So is your nose, Benny!"

Benny had paint splattered on his overalls. There was a dab in his hair and a bright yellow spot on his nose. He rubbed his face.

"It's okay, Benny. It will wash off your nose," Violet said. "I was just practicing on this wall. I will paint my sign on the door when it is dry. Then I will use all the right colors."

"But what about that?" Benny asked. He pointed to Violet's painting. "Now there are yellow strawberries on the wall. That doesn't look right."

"I'll show you!" Violet took a large brush and painted over her picture. It disappeared in a minute.

"I'm going to do that too!" Benny painted a small dog on the wall. "It's Watch!" he cried. The cat mewed. "Don't be scared, Sunny. It's just a picture. Besides, Watch would never hurt you. He is a friendly dog."

Benny took a big brush and painted over Watch. "Now he's gone!"

Henry was standing on a ladder. "Look at mine!" he called. He had painted a baseball player holding a bat. Henry was very good at sports.

Soon, the children were painting pictures all over the walls. As soon as they finished each one, they painted over it. They made it into a guessing game. It was easy to guess what Violet had painted. Her art was very lifelike. Some of Benny's pictures were just a jumble of lines that made everyone laugh. "It's a rocket ship landing on the moon," he said of one of his pictures. "See? Here is the astronaut. He is flying."

Jessie smiled at her little brother. He had only made a yellow circle and a yellow rectangle. But Benny had a very big imagination.

Drawing pictures and painting over them made the work fun. Time flew by quickly.

Henry was just moving his ladder when he heard shouting outside.

"Helloooo! Hellooo! Anybody still in there?"

"It sounds like Mr. Carroll," Jessie said, rushing to open the door.

"Hello, children," Mr. Carroll said. "I didn't want to knock. The door still looks wet." He looked around the room. "You've done a great job so far. Would you like some help?"

"Yes, thank you," Henry said.

"I've brought something that should make the work go quickly." Mr. Carroll had a small machine. It had a long wand attached to it. He poured paint into the machine.

"Okay, Benny," Mr. Carroll said. "I need your help. Can you push that button for me?"

When Benny pushed the button, a motor whirred. Paint sprayed from the wand onto the walls. In no time at all, Mr. Carroll had finished all the painting.

After all the brushes were cleaned, everyone stood and admired the room. It looked bright and cheerful.

"Now all we need is to fill up the shelves," Violet said.

Jessie noticed Benny's droopy eyes. He was yawning. "We should get home," she said. "It's late. Thank you for all your help, Mr. Carroll."

"It was my pleasure," Mr. Carroll said. "I'll walk out with you."

But when everyone went out into the alley, they were surprised.

Four bicycles were lying on the ground, and the tires were flat! Someone had cut holes in them all!

"Oh no!" Jessie cried. "Our bicycles! Who would do such a thing?"

Benny pulled a note from the basket on his bicycle. "St . . . stay away," he tried to sound out the words. "Min . . . Min . . ." He handed the paper to Jessie.

"STAY AWAY! Mind your own business!" Jessie read.

CHAPTER 4

Stolen Flyers

After dinner, Henry, Jessie, Violet, and Benny sat in chairs around the fireplace. Mrs. McGregor had set a fresh batch of ginger cookies and a pitcher of milk on the end table.

"It was nice of Mr. Carroll to give us a ride home," Violet said.

"He is very kind," Jessie agreed. She passed two large cookies to Benny.

Benny bit into the warm ginger cookie. "Do you think the shop put the new tires on our bikes yet?"

"I hope so," Henry said. "We'll need them to ride around town and distribute the flyers."

Violet sat with her sketch pad in her lap. She was drawing a picture of a turkey for the flyer. "We will need to be careful when we put the flyers up," she said. "Someone does not want us to help the food pantry."

"You're right, Violet," Henry said. "But who could it be?"

Jessie pulled out her notepad. When the Aldens were faced with a mystery, Jessie often took notes. "Do we have any clues at all?" she asked.

"What about the man who knocked into Mr. Grayson in the street?" Violet asked. "I don't think it was an accident. And he seemed very angry."

"I wish we had gotten a better look at him," Jessie said. "I agree that he pushed Mr. Grayson on purpose." She tapped her pencil on her pad. "Anyone else?"

"What about the lady who owns Harvest Restaurant, Ms. Matthews?" Henry said. "She called Mr. Grayson a liar right in the

Green Fields restaurant."

Benny took a long drink from his glass. He had a big milk mustache. "That's right!" he said. "She called Mr. Grayson a fraud. What is that?"

"A fraud is someone who pretends to be something that he is not," Jessie explained.

"Do you think Mr. Grayson is pretending, Jessie?" Benny asked.

Jessie watched the fire crackle in the fireplace. "I don't know, Benny. Mr. Grayson is Grandfather's friend, and he seems very sincere."

"We will have to keep our eyes open tomorrow when we are in town," Henry said. "Maybe we will find more clues."

The next day, Grandfather drove the children to the bike shop. Their bicycles all had brand-new tires. The first place they rode was to the office store. Violet handed her flyer to the lady at the copy center.

"Why, this is wonderful!" the lady said. "I didn't even know that we had a food pantry in town. I have a friend whose husband has been very sick. He has not been able to go to work for a long time. This food pantry could be just the thing to help her family."

"There is not much food in the food pantry yet," Jessie explained. "We are hoping that these flyers will help us get more donations."

"I'm sure they will," the lady said. She introduced herself. Her name was Colette. "It is a beautiful flyer. Whoever did it is a very good artist. It will get people's attention."

Violet's face colored. "Thank you," she said shyly. "I drew it. Do you know how much it will cost to copy the flyers?"

"It will not cost anything," Colette said. "I would like to donate these flyers to help the food pantry. And I will hang the first ones up right here in my store."

Henry, Jessie, Violet, and Benny thanked Colette. They put the flyers in their baskets and rode down Chestnut Street. Their first stop was at Mr. Carroll's hardware store. Mr. Carroll was happy to see them. "I'm so glad your bicycles are fixed," he said. He gave the children a roll of tape and told them to put up as many flyers as they wanted in his front windows.

The woman in the dress shop and the man in the bookstore were also very excited about the food pantry. They each helped to tape up flyers in their windows and on their front doors.

"Look!" Violet said. "The grocery store. That would be a perfect place for our flyers."

Higgins's Grocery Store had big display-windows. Outside, boxes were filled with pumpkins for sale. And there were beautiful mums in every color, all in a row. The children walked inside. The store was busy with shoppers.

"Excuse me," Jessie asked a cashier. "Would it be all right if we put these flyers up in your windows?"

Before the cashier could answer, a man came rushing over to the children. "What do you want in here?" he asked. "If you are not here to buy anything, you must leave right now."

"We're sorry to disturb you," Jessie said.

"We were just wondering if we could put these flyers in your window."

"Flyers? Let me see those." The man grabbed the stack of flyers from Jessie's hand. His face seemed to grow dark when he read the flyer. "I'll think about it," he said. He stormed off into his office. He slammed the door so hard that his brown hat and scarf fell from the hook on the back of the door.

The cashier looked at the Aldens. She shrugged. "Sorry, kids. That was Mr. Higgins. He owns this grocery store."

The children walked back outside to their bicycles.

"He took all my flyers," Jessie said. "And I don't think he's going to hang them up."

"I don't think so, either," Henry said. "But why would he be angry about the flyers?"

Henry, Jessie, Violet, and Benny continued down the street. They stopped in many stores and offices. Everyone was very kind and very excited about the food pantry. Mrs. James in the shoe store hung up the flyers and also gave Henry twenty dollars for the food pantry.

Anthony in the tailor shop even offered to donate clothes to anyone who needed them.

"The people in Greenfield are very generous," Jessie said. The children were standing at the end of the street. Right in front of them was Harvest Restaurant—the restaurant owned by Ms. Matthews.

"Do you think we should go in there?" Violet asked.

"I don't know," Henry said. "Ms. Matthews does not seem to like Mr. Grayson."

Violet looked thoughtful. "I think that we should go in," she said. "Maybe Ms. Matthews does not like Mr. Grayson, but she should not be against a food pantry. And if she is, maybe we can try to find out why."

Everyone agreed, and they went inside Harvest Restaurant.

"We ate here before," Benny said. "They have good food." Benny stood by the case that held lots of delicious desserts. There were pies and cakes and puddings with whipped cream on the top.

The hostess greeted them. "Would you

like a table?" she asked.

"Yes!" Benny said before anyone else could answer. "I'm starved!"

Henry, Jessie, and Violet were surprised. Jessie was about to object. They had not come in to eat. They only wanted to ask about the flyers. But it was lunch time. And Benny seemed so eager. The children followed the hostess to a table by the front window.

Benny leaned forward. "You're not mad at me, are you?" he whispered.

"Of course not," Jessie said. "But we were surprised. I thought we would go to Green Fields for lunch and tell Mr. Grayson about the flyers."

"I know," Benny said. "But Ms. Matthews will be happy that we are eating in her restaurant. Maybe she will give us some clues!"

"That's very smart, Benny," Henry said.

"And it smells good in here, too," Benny admitted. "And all those pies and cakes looked so delicious. My stomach knew it was the right thing to do!"

After the waitress brought their food, the children asked her if they could see Ms. Matthews. They wanted to ask her about putting the flyers in her restaurant. Very soon, they saw Ms. Matthews hurrying up to their table. She had an angry look on her face.

Benny took a big bite of his hamburger. "Your food is delicious!" he said. "I could eat ten of these hamburgers!"

The look on Ms. Matthews's face changed. She smiled at Benny. "I'm glad you like it," she said. "How can I help you children?"

Violet showed Ms. Matthews the flyers. She asked if they could put some around the restaurant.

"No! No flyers! Do you see any signs or flyers anywhere in my restaurant? No! People do not like to look at such things when they come here. They want to relax and have a nice meal." Ms. Matthews tried to take the flyers from Violet's hand.

Violet did not let go. She handed one flyer to Ms. Matthews, but she kept the rest. "We could put them outside," she said. "It would not bother anyone's meal out there."

Ms. Matthews read the flyer. Then she crumpled it in her hand. "Look, kids. You are being duped. Brian Grayson doesn't care about any food pantry. I've seen that place. No one goes there. No one is helped. He collects food and he uses it in his restaurant. He wants to drive me out of business!"

"But Mr. Grayson is—" Violet tried to explain that the food pantry was just getting started. But Ms. Matthews cut her off.

"And now I hear he is having a free Thanksgiving dinner for anyone who shows up at his restaurant!" Ms. Matthews tossed the crumpled flyer onto the table.

"But that's nice, isn't it?" Benny asked.

Ms. Matthews shook her head. "Nice? I have been open for business for Thanksgiving for twenty years. I have worked hard to have a good business. Now Brian Grayson is trying to ruin my restaurant. He is not nice. You children should beware. Brian Grayson is sneaky." Ms. Matthews walked slowly back into her kitchen.

"Do you really think Mr. Grayson is sneaky?" Benny asked.

Henry looked out the window. Green Fields restaurant was right across the street. "I don't know," he answered. "Mr. Grayson seems like a good man to me. But maybe he does want Harvest Restaurant to go out of business. Then more people would eat at Green Fields."

Jessie had pulled out her notebook. She was writing down the things that Ms. Matthews had said. "But aren't there enough customers for *both* restaurants?" she asked.

Violet looked around Harvest Restaurant. Ms. Matthews was stopping at tables and talking with customers. She picked up a napkin that had fallen on the floor. She helped a waitress who was struggling with a heavy tray. "Ms. Matthews cares a lot about her restaurant," Violet said. "I didn't know she had been working here for twenty years. That is a long time."

"Look!" Jessie said. She pointed out the window. Mr. Grayson was walking down the street. He was carrying a very big bag. It looked heavy. He turned to stare at Harvest Restaurant before he opened the door to Green Fields. He suddenly seemed surprised. Then he quickly went into his restaurant.

"I think Mr. Grayson saw us eating in here," Jessie said.

"But what's wrong with that?" Benny asked. "The food is good here."

Jessie sighed. "There's nothing wrong with it, I suppose," she said. "But Mr. Grayson and Ms. Matthews are competitors."

Benny bit into his last french fry. "I think I get it," he said. "It's like a game. Because we ate lunch here today, Ms. Matthews won."

"Something like that," Jessie said.

After lunch, the children headed across the street to Green Fields. Mr. Grayson seemed very pleased with the flyers that Violet had made. He taped them up all around his restaurant.

"Your flyers have already worked," Mr. Grayson told Violet. "Someone saw them and made a wonderful donation. Come back in the kitchen and I will show you."

The children followed Mr. Grayson into the kitchen. It was very busy. Cooks in white hats were shaking sizzling pans over a fire. Waiters and waitresses were arranging food on the plates. Everyone seemed to be in a hurry. Jessie held Benny's hand as they walked through the rush of workers.

Mr. Grayson stopped in front of a large silver door. "This is a freezer," he said. "I hope you don't mind the cold."

Benny's eyes grew large. "A freezer?" he said. "It is almost as big as my bedroom!"

Mr. Grayson laughed. "Yes," he said. "It is big. It is called a walk-in freezer. Because we have so much food at the restaurant, we need to have a lot of space in our freezer."

"What's that?" Benny cried, shivering. He pointed at a huge turkey wrapped in plastic. It was so cold, his breath came out in little clouds.

"That's what I wanted to show you," Mr. Grayson said. "It is a donation. Mr. Beckett, who runs a farm near Greenfield, has donated this turkey. He saw Violet's flyer and he wanted to help. He couldn't find the food pantry, so he called me. He said that you helped solve a mystery on his farm about a pumpkin head ghost! You kids sure seem to get involved in a lot of mysteries."

"That is the largest turkey I have ever seen," Henry said. "It must be very heavy."

"I was planning on cooking this turkey for Thanksgiving dinner," Mr. Grayson said. "I am going to have a free dinner at the restaurant for the needy. It will be a good way to start off our food pantry and let everyone know that no one in Greenfield should ever have to be hungry."

"That's a wonderful idea," Violet said. But she knew that Ms. Matthews did not feel the same way.

Back in the kitchen, Violet saw a recycling bin filled with used glass jars. "Could we take these jars?" she asked. "We would like to make them into donation jars and place them on the counters in the stores on Main Street."

"That is a terrific idea," Mr. Grayson said. "Take all that you need."

The children carefully put the jars into bags and placed them in the baskets of their bicycles.

"We better get home quickly," Henry said. "I think a storm is coming."

A cold wind had begun to blow. Dark clouds were swirling in the sky. The children pedaled quickly down Main Street. The street was mostly empty. Just as they were about to turn toward home, they saw a man wearing a dark brown scarf and a hat. He was hurrying down the street, ripping Violet's flyers off each window that he passed!

CHAPTER 5

A Giant Flying Turkey

Henry, Jessie, Violet, and Benny had gotten wet in the storm. They changed into warm, dry clothes when they got home. Mrs. McGregor made steaming hot chocolate and put some pumpkin bread into the oven.

"You poor children. You must have been freezing!" she said. "What do you have in those wet bags?"

"These are used jars, Mrs. McGregor," Jessie said. "We are going to clean them out and make them into donation jars."

Mrs. McGregor peeked into the bags. "They need cleaning, for sure!" she said. She filled a tub with hot, soapy water. She dumped the jars into the water. "I would like to help. I will clean the jars, and you children can dry them and decorate them."

While the children drank their hot chocolate, Mrs. McGregor used a brush and scrubbed the jars clean. Henry, Jessie, and Benny dried the jars while Violet sketched a small sign to place on them.

"I was thinking about something that Mr. Grayson said." Violet shaded in the words in her sketch. "He said that Mr. Beckett could not find the food pantry."

"We couldn't find it, either," Henry said. "If it weren't for Benny, we would not have known where to look."

Jessie rubbed a smudge from one of the jars. "So even if we get a lot of food to put on the shelves in the food pantry, how will anyone find it?"

"That's what I was thinking, too," Violet said. She turned her sketch pad around so her sister and brothers could see it.

"It's a turkey!" Benny cried. "It's really good, Violet."

"Thank you," Violet said. "I thought maybe the turkey could help people find the food pantry."

Benny's hand was stuck inside a small jar. He struggled to slip it out. "But how can a turkey do that? It is a just a little picture."

Henry smiled at Violet. "I think I know what Violet is thinking. We can go back to the copy center. They can make giant signs from small drawings."

"Yes!" Violet said. "We could get the turkey made into a big stand-up sign. Then we could place it on the street outside the alley."

"Everyone would see that!" Jessie said.

"A giant turkey on Chestnut Street! This is going to be so cool!" Benny said.

The next day, the children placed all their donation jars carefully back into their bicycle baskets. They rode into town. Their first stop was the copy center. Colette was at work behind the counter. She loved the idea of the giant turkey sign.

"It might take me an hour or so to make it, kids," she said. "Do you think you could come back a little later?"

"Of course," Jessie said. "Thank you so much."

The children rode down the street and stopped in all the same stores as yesterday. They left donation jars with all the kind shopkeepers. They did not stop in Higgins's Grocery Store or in Harvest Restaurant.

"Do you have any more of those flyers?" asked Mrs. James in the shoe store. "Someone ripped them off the outside of my window yesterday. Who would do such a thing?"

Violet explained that someone was trying to stop the food pantry from opening. They did not know who it was.

"I will keep my eyes open," Mrs. James said. "I'll let you kids know if I see anything suspicious."

The children rode back to the office store. They had a few jars left in their baskets.

Colette was waiting for them. She had a big smile on her face.

Benny raced across the store. He shouted. "Wow! Violet, your turkey has grown into a giant!"

Even Violet was surprised. Her turkey was six feet tall! It could stand all by itself. It held a sign with an arrow that said, *Food Pantry This Way.*

"Thank you so much!" Jessie said. "We could not ask for a better sign. Now everyone will know where the food pantry is."

"I am very happy to help," Colette said. "If you need any more signs or flyers, please let me know."

Henry carried the giant turkey out of the store. All the customers watched, laughing.

"Let's leave our bicycles here," Henry said. "We'll set up the giant turkey in front of the alley, and then we will come back for them."

Everyone outside stopped to see the turkey being carried down the street. Mr. Carroll came out of his hardware store.

"That's quite a sign you've got!" he said.

"Would you like some help setting it up?"

"Yes, thanks," Henry said.

Henry set the turkey at the front of the alley. The arrow pointed down the alley to the food pantry. Suddenly, a gust of wind picked the turkey up and it began to fly!

"Whoa! Come back, Tom!" Benny called. He ran after the turkey and grabbed its wing. "I got it!"

Henry and Benny brought the turkey back.

"Tom?" Mr. Carroll asked.

"I named him Tom," Benny said. "I didn't know turkeys could fly."

Mr. Carroll laughed. "Mr. Tom Turkey needs to be tied down to his spot. I will be right back."

Mr. Carroll brought some heavy bags of sand and some twine. He poked a few holes in the bottom of the sign and he tied the sign to the sand bags. "This turkey won't be escaping anymore!" he said.

Tom the turkey seemed very secure. A crowd of people gathered to look at him.

"A food pantry?" asked one woman.

"I didn't know Greenfield had a food pantry. What a wonderful idea. I have a friend who just had a new baby. She could really use some help. This would be wonderful for her."

Jessie explained how Mr. Grayson was trying to gather donations to get the food pantry started.

"I saw the flyers!" one man said. "Now I know where the food pantry is. I will make sure to tell all my friends." He handed a ten-dollar bill to Jessie. "This is so you can buy some food for the pantry," he said. "It is wonderful that you kids are helping."

"Thank you!" Jessie said.

More people in the crowd opened their purses and their wallets. They gave a lot of money to Henry and Jessie. The food pantry would soon have lots of nutritious food on its shelves.

"Your turkey is a great success, Violet!" Henry said.

Just then, Mr. Grayson came hurrying down the street. He stopped quickly when he saw the giant turkey. "Wow. What a turkey! I saw a crowd near the alley and I thought something was wrong," he said. "I was worried that someone was trying to hurt the food pantry again!"

"No," Henry said. "Everything is fine. Here is money that people have already donated." He put the bills into Mr. Grayson's hands.

Mr. Grayson was very surprised. For a moment, he couldn't speak. "Th-thank you," he finally stammered gratefully. "Let's go inside."

Mr. Grayson opened the door to the food pantry. The bright lights and bold yellow walls made it a very warm, inviting room. He took the children into the back office. He showed them the box where he kept the money he was saving to buy food for the pantry. "I hardly had anything in here until today," he said. "You children have done a wonderful job."

"We put donation jars out today, too," Benny said. "So we can get more money soon."

Mr. Grayson took all the money and put it in his pocket. "I am going to put this money in the bank for now," he said.

They all walked back out of the office. Mr. Grayson looked around the pantry. "It is really starting to look like a real food pantry," he said. "Soon, people who need help will be shopping here for their families. You children are doing a wonderful thing."

Mr. Grayson locked up the pantry and headed back to his restaurant.

"Goodbye, Tom!" Benny said to the giant cardboard turkey. "I hope he doesn't get lonely out here by himself."

A group of children ran up to Tom the turkey. They giggled and touched his giant cardboard feathers.

"I don't think Tom will get a chance to be lonely," Jessie said. "He's becoming very popular in Greenfield!"

When the Aldens got back to the office center, their bicycles where lying on the ground. Broken glass was all around!

"Oh no!" Violet said. "Our bikes must have blown over in the wind. And all the jars have fallen out and broken."

Henry bent down to take a look at the glass. Jessie held Benny's hand. She did not want him to get cut on the sharp glass.

"It wasn't the wind," Henry said. "The jars in my basket were closed tightly in a bag. I tied the knot myself. The wind is strong, but it cannot untie knots."

The children looked up and down the street. They did not see anyone who looked suspicious. After they cleaned up the mess, they went back to check on the turkey. Many people were still stopping to admire the giant bird. Some had walked down the alley to see where the food pantry was located.

"Are you sure he will be safe here all night by himself?" Benny asked. "I don't want to leave him. I could stay and take care of him."

Jessie laughed. "He's just a cardboard turkey, Benny. He will be fine. Mr. Carroll did a good job of setting him up. Mr. Tom Turkey is nice and secure."

Benny wasn't so sure. As they got on their bicycles to ride home, Benny saw someone quickly duck into a doorway to hide. He thought the person looked familiar, but he didn't know who it was. But Henry, Jessie, and Violet were getting ahead of him. Benny pedaled hard and quickly caught up with his brother and sisters.

CHAPTER 6

A Clue in the Alley

"In celebration of Violet's great idea!" said Mrs. McGregor as she set a plate of pancakes on the table. Each pancake was shaped like a turkey!

"How did you do that, Mrs. McGregor?" asked Benny. "How can a pancake look like a turkey?" He scooped several of the thick golden turkeys onto his plate.

Mrs. McGregor laughed. "It's not so hard, Benny. I found a turkey mold in the store the other day. I thought it was a cute idea."

"It's a delicious idea! I'm going to give mine some eyes." Benny put raisins on the turkey's face. "Now he's going for a swim!" Benny dunked the turkey in a pool of maple syrup.

Grandfather laughed. "I've never seen anyone enjoy food as much as you do, Benny."

Just then, the phone rang, and Grandfather left the room.

Jessie noticed that Henry was holding his fork in a funny way. "What's wrong, Henry?" she asked.

Henry looked at his finger. "Just a small cut," he said. "I think when we were cleaning up last night, I got a piece of glass stuck in my finger. It's just a little sore."

"That's terrible!" Violet said.

"Yes," Jessie agreed. "I just don't understand why someone would try to hurt the food pantry. Who could be against helping those who are hungry?"

"Ms. Matthews is against the food pantry,"

Violet said. "She does not even believe that Mr. Grayson is trying to open a food pantry. She thinks Mr. Grayson is trying to put her out of business and steal her customers."

"That's true," Jessie said. "And Mr. Higgins also seems to be angry about the food pantry. But I can't figure out why he would feel that way. Mr. Grayson is not trying to put him out of business."

Benny ate the head of his turkey. It made him remember something. "I saw someone last night," he said.

"What do you mean?" asked Violet.

"When we were saying good-bye to Tom the turkey, someone was sneaking up. When I looked up to see who it was, he jumped into a doorway to hide."

"That's strange," said Henry. "Do you think it was Mr. Higgins or Ms. Matthews?"

"I don't know," Benny said. "I couldn't really tell. I did not see the person's face. There was something that seemed familiar about the person, but I don't know what it was."

Grandfather came back to the table. "Sorry about that, children. But that was an important call. Do you remember my friend, Mr. Tipton?"

"Oh yes," said Jessie. "Doesn't he own the movie theater?"

"That's right, he does. He saw Violet's flyers and he would like to help. He is going to have a night at the movies for the food pantry. Admission is free as long as you bring some canned goods for the pantry."

"What a wonderful idea!" Jessie said.

Grandfather opened up the newspaper. "Look. There is already an advertisement in the paper for the special movie night."

The children gathered around. It was a big advertisement. Everyone in Greenfield was sure to see it. It was for a new, popular movie called *The Secret Under the Stairs*.

"Can we go, Grandfather?" asked Benny.

"Of course you can go, Benny," Grandfather said. "You will have to stand at the door to help collect all those canned goods! I just hope the movie isn't too scary for you."

Benny jumped back from the table. "I'm not afraid of anything!" he said. "I won't get scared by a movie!"

After cleaning the breakfast dishes, Henry, Jessie, Violet, and Benny rode their bicycles into town. They wanted to thank Mr. Tipton and tell Mr. Grayson about the special movie night.

"Can we stop and see Tom the turkey first?" asked Benny.

"Sure," Henry said. "We have to pass right by him. It's just up around the corner."

But when the children turned the corner, they did not see what they expected.

"He's gone!" Benny cried. "I knew it! We should never have left him alone!"

"Maybe he blew away," Violet said. "It was quite windy last night."

Henry jumped off his bicycle. The bags of sand were right where Mr. Carroll had left them. Henry lifted up the string that was attached to the bags. He looked at it closely. "Someone cut this string," he said. "Tom the turkey did not blow away. He was stolen!"

Benny ran down the alley. "Tom!" he called. "Tom! Where are you?"

When Benny came back, he was carrying Sunny, the yellow cat. "I couldn't find Tom, but Sunny was in the alley."

Jessie petted the little cat. "She must be hungry. And that gives me an idea," she said. "We can go to Higgins's Grocery Store to buy some cat food for Sunny. While we're there, we could look around to see if Tom the turkey is somewhere in the store."

"Do you really think Mr. Higgins would steal Violet's sign?" Henry asked.

"I don't know," Jessie answered. "But it is worth investigating."

Henry, Jessie, Violet, and Benny rode their bicycles to Higgins's Grocery Store. They carefully placed their bicycles on the side of the building so they would not be in anyone's way.

"I don't see Tom the turkey out front," Benny said.

"If I stole a big turkey," Henry said, "I would hide it in the back. I will go look in the alley behind the store."

"We will check inside," Jessie said.

In the store, they split up. Jessie and Benny went up and down the first six aisles. Violet looked over the last six aisles. She ran into Mr. Higgins in the frozen food section.

"What are you doing here?" he asked gruffly.

Violet was surprised. "I'm looking for . . ." she almost said "turkey" but remembered at the last moment. "I'm here for some cat food," she answered.

Mr. Higgins glared at Violet. "Cat food is not in the frozen foods," he said. "It is in the pet food aisle."

"Of course," Violet said. "That is where I am going."

Just then, there was a commotion in the back of the store. Mr. Higgins glanced at Violet, then hurried toward the noise. Violet followed.

Mr. Higgins pushed through the swinging doors into the storage area. Benny was sitting on the floor. Boxes were scattered all around him.

"What is going on here?" Mr. Higgins shouted.

Jessie helped Benny to his feet. She brushed him off.

"I'm sorry," Benny said. "I thought I saw a turkey up there." He pointed to the top of a high shelf. A colorful cardboard turkey sat next to some boxes. It was not as big as Violet's turkey. It held a sign that advertised stuffing. "And then I accidentally backed into these boxes."

"You should not be back here," Mr. Higgins said. "This is not an area for customers. You could have been hurt." He turned to Jessie. "You should do a better job of watching your little brother."

"We're sorry," Jessie said. She squeezed Benny's hand. His eyes were turning red.

"I must ask you to leave the store," Mr. Higgins said. "For some reason, we are having an extra-busy day today. We are working very hard to keep our shelves stocked with canned goods. And you children are causing trouble."

Outside, Benny rubbed his eyes. "I'm sorry, Jessie," he said. "I didn't mean to get us in trouble. I just wanted to peek in the back. I thought I saw Tom the turkey."

"It's all right," Jessie said. "You should not have gone back there. But you didn't mean any harm. And nothing was damaged."

Henry came around the corner. He did not find Tom the turkey in the alley. "But look at this," he said. Henry held up two long pieces of string. "This looks just like the string Mr. Carroll used to tie the turkey sign to the sand bags."

Jessie took the string from Henry. "I think you are right, Henry. It does look the same. But Mr. Higgins may use the same kind of string in his store."

"He might," Henry answered. "But it is a coincidence."

"But if the string is there, where is the turkey?" asked Violet. "It is too big to hide in a trash can and it was not in the store."

Just then, a lady in a red jacket and a dark pair of slacks walked up to the children. She was carrying a notebook and a pen. "Are you the Aldens?" she asked.

"Yes," Jessie answered.

"My name is Gail Sweeney. I am a reporter for the *Greenfield Times*. We had an anonymous call today. Someone told us that you are helping to set up a food pantry in Greenfield and that your turkey sign is missing."

The children looked surprised. "We have been helping," Henry said. "But it is Mr. Grayson from the Green Fields restaurant who is setting up the food pantry."

"Can you tell me about the giant turkey sign that is missing?" asked the reporter. "I think that would make a great story for our paper."

"His name is Tom!" Benny said. "Someone stole him! Can you write in the paper that we want him back?"

The reporter smiled. "Of course I will," she said.

"Violet drew the turkey," Jessie explained. "She is a wonderful artist. Colette from the copy center made Violet's turkey into a big sign. She was very kind. She donated the sign."

"And why did you need such a big sign?" asked the reporter.

"The food pantry is at the end of a small alley," Henry explained. "Most people did not know it was there. We thought a big sign would help everyone find the food pantry."

"I see." The reporter jotted notes in her notebook. "Do you think that perhaps the sign blew away?"

"No," Henry replied. "Mr. Carroll from the hardware store has been helping with the food pantry, also. He tied the sign down. It was very secure. Someone cut the string."

"Do you have any idea who could have stolen the turkey sign?" asked the reporter.

The children looked at one another, but they did not answer. They had suspects, but they had no proof. They did not want to accuse anyone.

"C'mon kids," said the reporter. "You can tell me. I would like to interview this person if you know who it is."

"We're sorry," Jessie said. "We do not know. But we know something else for your story."

"What's that?" the reporter asked.

"Tomorrow night there will be a free movie at the movie theater. You only have to bring some canned goods for admission. All the donations will go to the food pantry. Can you put that in your story?"

The reporter smiled. "You care a lot about this food pantry, don't you?"

Jessie nodded.

"I will put it in my story," she said. "And I will come to movie myself!"

The reporter asked each of the children to spell their names. "You will all be in the newspaper tomorrow." She thanked them and left for her office.

Benny ran down the sidewalk, away from his siblings.

Jessie called after him. "Benny, wait! Where are you going? You forgot your bike!"

"I'm going to be in the newspaper!" Benny called. "I have to go tell Grandfather. I am going to be famous!"

CHAPTER 7

A Mysterious Visitor

"I am very proud of you, children," Grandfather said. He spread the newspaper on the breakfast table. The story about the food pantry was right on the front page!

"The Gr . . . Greeet . . . Turkey He . . ." Benny tried to sound out the words in the headline. "Henry, can you help me?"

"That was a good try, Benny," Henry said. "Some of those words are hard. The headline reads, 'The Great Turkey Heist.'"

"What is a heist?" Benny asked.

"It is a robbery," Grandfather answered. "It means that someone stole your great turkey sign."

Benny was leaning over the newspaper article trying to find words that he could read. Suddenly, he started to jump up and down. "Look! There's my name!" he cried. "It says 'Benny Alden.' I am in the newspaper! I'm famous!"

Everyone laughed. Mrs. McGregor set a platter of waffles and a pitcher of milk on the table. "Here is something to fill up your famous stomach," she said.

As the children ate, Grandfather read the story in the newspaper aloud. It was a very good story. It gave facts about the food pantry. It also discussed the mysterious disappearance of the turkey sign. And, just as the reporter promised, the story mentioned the movie night.

"Wow! We're going to get lots of donations for the food pantry tonight!" Benny said.

"Yes, I think you are right, Benny," Jessie said. "Oh, and let's not forget—we promised

Mr. Tipton that we would go to the theater early to help get ready."

"I have a meeting this afternoon in town," Grandfather said. "I will give you a ride."

When Grandfather dropped them off in town, Mr. Tipton was outside his theater. He was on a ladder. "Hello!" he called. When he waved at the children, the ladder shook.

Henry quickly grasped the ladder. He held it steady.

"Glad to see you, children. I'm just finishing up here. I will be down shortly. Can you hand me those letters?" Mr. Tipton asked.

A few large black letters sat on the ground. Benny picked up a *T.* "Wow! This letter is almost as big as me."

"The letters need to be big so everyone can see them," Mr. Tipton said. "This is called a marquee. I change the letters every week to advertise the movies." Mr. Tipton placed the last few letters on the marquee. He climbed down and looked up at his theater.

"It looks wonderful," Violet said.

"What does it say?" Benny asked.

"*The Secret Under the Stairs*," Jessie read. "Starring Marla White. And on the other side it says 'Greenfield Food Pantry Night Tonight.'"

"I am expecting a big crowd," Mr. Tipton said. "I think everyone in town read the story in the paper this morning. My phone has been ringing off the hook."

"That's wonderful," Jessie said.

"Why don't you children come inside so I can show you around?" Mr. Tipton held open the door to his theater. Henry carried the ladder inside.

First, Mr. Tipton took the children into his office. Movie posters decorated the walls. Stacks of tickets sat on the desk.

"That's a lot of tickets!" Benny said.

Mr. Tipton laughed. "Yes. Movie theaters always need to have a lot of tickets. You will have to give one ticket to each person who brings a donation for the food pantry. Let's bring the tickets up front to the booth."

Mr. Tipton took a key from his pocket and unlocked the sales booth. It was small inside.

There was one tall chair. A dark curtain hung in front of the curved window. Mr. Tipton pushed the curtain back. Suddenly, the room was filled with light.

Jessie helped Benny climb up onto the chair. "I can see the whole street from here!" he said.

Mr. Tipton opened a metal panel. He put the tickets into the ticket machine. "Okay, Benny," he said. "Push that button and see what happens."

Benny pushed the button on the desk. An orange ticket popped out of a slot. "Cool!" Benny said. He pulled the ticket off.

"When the ticket comes out, you slide it through the opening to the customer." Mr. Tipton showed the children the small opening in the window.

"But the canned goods will not fit in through this little opening," Benny said. "Only money could fit through there."

"We will set bins up outside by the door," Mr. Tipton said. "After the customer puts in his or her donation, we will give them a ticket to the movie."

"Do we have any bins?" Jessie asked.

"Yes. I have been collecting some. Come upstairs to the projection room, and I will show you."

The children followed Mr. Tipton up a narrow staircase. He opened an old wooden door. He pulled a cord and a dim light went on.

"I have always wanted to see the projection room," Violet said.

"But what do you do up here?" Benny asked.

"This is where we play the movies, Benny!" Mr. Tipton said.

"But I don't see any movies. I don't even see a DVD player." Benny looked all around the room.

"Here are the movies," Mr. Tipton said. He walked over to a shelf that held large tins. "Inside each tin is a reel of film. Here, Violet. Would you like to carry this over to the projector? You can help me set up the film for tonight."

"Thank you!" Violet said. "I would love to."

While Mr. Tipton and Violet were setting up the film in the projector, Benny was investigating the rest of the room. He found a small window. Jessie boosted him up so that he could look through.

"I can see the whole movie theater from up here!" he cried.

Mr. Tipton laughed. "Yes," he said. "When I turn on the projector tonight, it will shine the movie through that little window and onto the screen. That is how a movie gets shown at a movie theater."

Suddenly, Benny saw something moving down below. The theater was dark, but he was certain that a person had just run across the stage in front of the screen.

"Mr. Tipton," he said. "There is someone else in the theater. Is that okay?"

"What?" Mr. Tipton rushed to the little window. "No one else should be in here! I don't see anyone," he said.

"Are you sure you saw someone, Benny?" asked Henry.

"Yes, I'm sure," Benny said. "It is dark, but

I know I saw a person down by the screen."

Everyone rushed down the narrow stairs. Suddenly, they all heard a door bang shut. Mr. Tipton hurried into the lobby. "Someone was definitely here," he said. "But it does not look like anything was stolen."

Mr. Tipton and the children checked the whole theater. They made sure all the doors were now shut and locked. They did not see any damage.

"Why would someone come in an empty theater and just run around?" Jessie said. "It is odd."

"It *is* odd," Mr. Tipton said. "We will have to be careful. I did not mention this earlier because I thought it was just a prank. But someone called the theater today and demanded that I call off the special food pantry night."

The children looked very surprised. "Did you recognize the voice?" Henry asked.

"No," Mr. Tipton said. "It could have been anybody."

"We will have to carefully watch the bins

tonight," Henry said. "Someone may try to take the donations."

"I think you are right, Henry," Mr. Tipton said.

"I can do it!" Benny said. "I am a good detective."

"I am sure you would be good at the door," Mr. Tipton said. "But I also need help at the snack counter. I was hoping you could do that."

"Oh boy!" Benny said. "I sure can. I love snacks!"

Jessie laughed. "Mr. Tipton wants help selling the snacks, Benny, not eating them."

Mr. Tipton took Benny behind the counter. He showed him how to make the popcorn in the big popcorn-popping machine. Benny scooped the corn kernels from a bin. He stood on a stool and poured the kernels into the machine. Then he pushed the button to turn on the popper. Soon, the whole place smelled wonderful.

Mr. Tipton gave each of the children a bag of the warm popcorn and a cup of lemonade.

A phone began to ring and Mr. Tipton hurried to his office.

The children went into the theater to eat. They sat in a row in the soft, velvety seats.

"This popcorn is delicious," Violet said.

"I made it!" Benny said proudly.

Jessie smiled. "It is the best popcorn I've ever had."

"Can you tell us anything about the person you saw, Benny?" asked Henry. "Are you sure you don't know who it could have been?"

Benny shook his head sadly. "I don't know," he said. "It was very dark. The person looked mostly like a shadow. I could not see a face."

"Could you tell if it was a man or a woman?" asked Violet.

"No," Benny said. "But the shadow was big. I think it was probably a man."

"Was he wearing a hat?" asked Jessie. She remembered the rude man who knocked into Mr. Grayson on the street. He had been wearing a brown hat.

"No," Benny said. "I did not see a hat."

Jessie pulled out her notebook. She wrote

down everything that had happened at the theater. She tapped her pencil on her book. "Who could it have been?" she wondered.

"It could have been Mr. Higgins," Benny said. "He does not like the food pantry."

"It could have been Ms. Matthews, too," Henry said. "She does not even believe that the food pantry will ever open," Henry said. "She thinks Mr. Grayson is just being sneaky."

"But why would either Ms. Matthews or Mr. Higgins sneak into the theater during the day?" asked Violet.

"It makes no sense," Jessie said.

The children sat quietly for a few moments thinking about the mystery.

"There are a lot of seats in this theater," Violet said. "If every person brings a donation, the food pantry shelves will be filled by tomorrow. We have to make sure there are no problems tonight."

CHAPTER 8

A Turkey at the Movies?

The line to get into the movie was very long. Violet sat in the booth and sold the tickets as fast as she could. Everyone seemed to have brought bagfuls of donations.

"What a wonderful idea!" one woman said.

"How kind of you to support the food pantry," a man said to Mr. Tipton. He dropped an armful of cereal boxes into the donation bins.

Henry and Mr. Tipton were very busy watching the bins. They soon became full.

Henry had to empty them several times. He put all the items in Mr. Tipton's office. Then he brought the empty bins back to the front of the theater.

Mr. Grayson came early and helped, as well. He shook Mr. Tipton's hand. "This is wonderful!" he said. "With all these donations, we will be able to open the food pantry in time for Thanksgiving."

Jessie and Benny were very busy behind the snack counter. They made a lot of popcorn and sold many candy bars. The line was growing long.

"Hi, kids!" Noreen, the waitress from Green Fields restaurant, stood in front of the counter. "Would you like some help back there?" she asked.

"Yes, please!" Jessie said.

Mr. Tipton stopped by the snack counter. "See anything suspicious?" he whispered to Jessie.

"No," she said. "But we have been so busy selling snacks. I am afraid we have not been watching as best we can."

"Keep up the good work," Mr. Tipton said. "I will donate half of all the money you make here tonight to the food pantry. So, the more you sell, the more I will donate."

Jessie smiled. "That is very generous," she said.

There were crowds of people standing in the lobby. They were talking excitedly about the new movie. Jessie started when she saw Ms. Matthews. She was standing in a corner watching all the excitement. Soon, she saw Jessie looking at her. She walked over to the snack counter.

"I see that you children did not take my advice," Ms. Matthews said. "You are still helping Mr. Grayson with the food pantry."

"Yes," Jessie said. "We believe that a food pantry in Greenfield is a very nice idea."

"You still believe that he is going to open up a food pantry?" Ms. Matthews shook her head. "I do not think so."

"So many people have come here tonight," Jessie said. "They all believe in the food pantry."

Ms. Matthews looked around the lobby. "The people of Greenfield are good and kind people," she said. "They are also very generous. But they do not know Mr. Grayson like I know him. He is sneaky. He was sneaking around Mr. Higgins's grocery store the other day. I saw him carrying a very big package out of the back alley. It was covered in plastic. When he saw me watching him, he hurried away. Do you know what he was doing?"

Jessie was surprised. "No. I do not."

Ms. Matthews started to walk away. She turned back to Jessie. "I do think a food pantry would be a good idea for our town. And I would like to be wrong about Mr. Grayson. But I don't think that I am."

Noreen handed a drink across the counter to a customer. Then she hurried over to Jessie. "What was that all about?" she asked. "Ms. Matthews is always so angry."

"She does not believe that there is really going to be a food pantry," Jessie said. "But she was not angry."

Noreen untied the apron that she had been wearing. "Is it okay if I leave?" she asked. "I need to go get ready."

"Get ready?" asked Jessie.

"I mean . . . get ready . . . get ready for the movie, of course!" Noreen handed the apron to Jessie.

"Oh yes," Jessie said. "I hope you enjoy the movie."

All the customers had filed into the theater. The lobby became quiet. Benny dramatically slid to the floor.

"Are you okay?" asked Jessie.

"That was hard work!" Benny said, hopping back to his feet. "I'm tired. But selling snacks is almost as fun as eating them."

Mr. Tipton, Henry, and Violet joined Jessie and Benny at the snack stand.

"Thank you for all your help," Mr. Tipton said. "This night is a big success because of you."

"It was fun!" Benny said. "I had never worked at a snack stand before."

"We collected so many donations," Henry

said. "You should see Mr. Tipton's office. It is piled high with canned goods and cereal boxes. All of the customers were very generous."

Jessie showed them the donation jar on the counter. It was filled with coins and dollar bills. "People even made donations at the snack counter," Jessie said. "Mr. Grayson will be very pleased. Where is he?"

"He said he would watch over the donations in my office," Mr. Tipton said. "We are trying to be very careful tonight."

Just then Ms. Sweeney, the reporter from the newspaper, walked up to the snack counter. "Congratulations, kids!" she said. "You have done a great job here. This movie theater is packed with people."

"Your article was very helpful," Henry said. "Thank you for printing it on the front page."

Ms. Sweeney smiled. "Just doing my job," she said. "I would like to write another article about this movie donation night," she said. "Can I interview you, Mr. Tipton?"

Mr. Tipton looked proud. "Of course," he said. "But I could not have done it without the Aldens. Let me show you my office. You will see how many donations we received tonight."

Everyone walked back toward Mr. Tipton's office. When they opened the door, they were shocked! All the stacks of donations that Henry had piled so neatly were knocked to the floor. The room was a mess.

Ms. Sweeney took out her camera. She took many pictures. "Who could have done this?" she asked.

The children and Mr. Tipton looked at one another. "We don't know," Mr. Tipton said.

"Do you think any of the food was stolen?" asked the reporter.

Mr. Tipton looked around the room. "I don't think so. But there was a donation jar on my desk and it is not there anymore. It was filled with money. Many people put dollars in it as they came into the theater. Someone has stolen it."

The reporter quickly scribbled notes in her notebook. Then she left. The children helped Mr. Tipton straighten up his office. He sat behind his desk.

"I am going to stay here," he said. "You children go enjoy the movie now. You deserve it."

Henry, Jessie, Violet, and Benny found seats at the very back of the theater. It seemed like an exciting movie. Something scary was hidden under the stairs. The actress walked carefully down the creaking stairs. Spiderwebs hung in front of her face. She carried a candle. Noises came from under the stairs.

Suddenly, Benny cried out. Jessie turned to him. "It's just a movie," she whispered. "Don't be scared."

"No," Benny said. "It's not just a movie! Look there!"

A loud gasp went up from the theater. Everyone saw it. It was Tom the turkey! He moved across the front of the movie screen.

"Hey!" someone called. "What's that giant

turkey doing? Get that out of here! We want to see the movie."

Henry, Jessie, Violet, and Benny jumped from their seats and raced to the front of the theater. But whoever had the turkey moved faster. Henry jumped up on the stage and ran to the edge of the screen. A door on the side opened and shut. Henry grabbed the doorknob, but the door was stuck. Someone was holding it from the other side! He could not get it open.

"Quick!" he said to his brother and sisters. "Let's go out the front door."

The Aldens ran through the lobby. They went outside and raced to the side of the theater. But no one was there.

"This is why I could not get the door open," Henry said. A chair was pushed up against the door. It was a wooden chair with green leaves painted on the sides.

"That chair looks familiar," Violet said.

"Violet is right. I have seen that chair somewhere, also," Jessie said. "But we should probably get back inside. The movie will be over soon, and we should help Mr. Tipton clean up."

After all the customers had left the theater, Mr. Tipton and the children walked to the screen. All the lights were on. They checked the stage and the screen. There was no damage. Most customers had thrown away their trash, but a few did not. The children picked up a few candy wrappers and popcorn boxes. Henry and Jessie swept the rows, and Mr. Tipton vacuumed the aisles. Soon, the theater was clean and ready for its next movie.

Everyone turned sharply when they heard the door open. But it was just Mr. Grayson. He seemed very happy. "We got so many wonderful donations!" he said. "My thanks to all of you."

"Yes," Mr. Tipton said, "but someone stole one of our donation jars. We could have had much more money for the food pantry."

"Oh well. I wouldn't worry about that. We'll get more. There will be another story in the paper tomorrow. People will want to read about the theft and about the giant turkey waddling across the movie screen," Mr. Grayson said. "C'mon kids, I will give you a ride home."

On the way to Grandfather's house, Mr. Grayson talked excitedly about the food pantry. He asked the children if they would help set up the donations on the shelves.

"Of course we will help," Jessie said.

"And I have more good news," Mr. Grayson said. "Some of the players from the Greenfield High football team want to help, also. At tomorrow's division championship game against Westtown High, everyone must bring a donation to get a ticket."

"That's wonderful," Jessie said.

"The football stadium is very large," Henry said. "And this is a big game for our team. If Greenfield High wins, they win the championship. There will be a lot of donations."

"Exactly!" Mr. Grayson said. "I think that several exciting things will happen tomorrow!" He winked at the children and dropped them by the front porch of Grandfather's house.

CHAPTER 9

Jessie Finds a Clue

After dinner, Henry, Jessie, Violet, and Benny sat around the fire in the living room.

Mrs. McGregor carried in a pitcher of warm apple cider and a plate of pumpkin bread fresh from the oven. "You children have had a long day," she said. "I thought you could use a snack before bed."

"Thank you, Mrs. McGregor," Henry said. "We would love a snack."

"Especially me!" Benny said, jumping to his feet.

"That is why I am cutting you an especially big piece of pumpkin bread!" Mrs. McGregor said. "I heard your stomach growling all the way from the kitchen."

Benny put his hand on his stomach. "It does that when I'm hungry," he said. "I can't help it."

"I know," Mrs. McGregor said. "And I am glad that I know how to make it quiet!" She handed Benny his plate and a fork.

The other children were hungry, as well, and took big slices of pumpkin bread. Benny lay on his stomach on the floor while he ate.

"Mr. Grayson sure seemed happy tonight," Benny said.

"He was happy," Violet said. "He was not even upset that the money in the donation jar was stolen."

"That's true," Henry said. "He wasn't surprised, either. When Mr. Tipton told him about the theft, he acted as if he already knew about it."

"And wasn't Mr. Grayson supposed to be watching Mr. Tipton's office?" Violet said.

"Yes," Henry said. "Mr. Tipton was nervous that something would happen. He said that Mr. Grayson was watching the office for him."

"Maybe he liked the movie too much and he forgot," Benny said.

"I don't remember seeing Mr. Grayson when the movie was over," Violet said. "He was missing for a while. He came back when the theater was cleaned up."

"It's a big movie theater," Henry said. "Mr. Grayson could have been somewhere else."

Jessie was writing a lot in her notebook. She told her sister and brothers about the conversation she had with Ms. Matthews at the snack stand.

"So Ms. Matthews was not angry about the food pantry idea?" asked Violet.

"No," Jessie replied. "She likes the food pantry idea. She just does not like Mr. Grayson. She insists that Mr. Grayson is sneaky. She said that she saw Mr. Grayson sneaking around behind Higgins's Grocery Store. She saw him carrying a very large package wrapped in plastic."

"So Ms. Matthews still believes that Mr. Grayson is not really going to open the food pantry?" asked Henry.

"That's right, Henry," Jessie said.

"Do you think Ms. Matthews could be right?" asked Violet. "Do you think we did all that work for nothing?"

Jessie stared into the fire. "Mr. Grayson seems very sincere about the food pantry. But I have to admit that something is not right. Where did Mr. Grayson go during the movie? Why didn't he watch the donations in the office? Why was he not upset that the money was stolen?"

"We should not forget that Ms. Matthews was at the theater, as well," Henry said. "She could have gone into the office and stolen the donations."

"I forgot to tell you!" Violet said. "Mr. Higgins was at the movie, too."

"That's right!" Henry said. "I saw him, also. He put a very large donation into the bin."

"That's odd," Jessie said. "Mr. Higgins hates the idea of a food pantry. Why would he make a large donation?"

"By making the donation, he got into the theater," Violet said. "If he was there, we must include him as a suspect. He could have gone into the office and stolen the money, too."

Benny jumped up from the floor. "And where is Tom the turkey? Why did he come to the movie and then run away? You should write those questions in your notebook, Jessie."

"I will, Benny," Jessie said. "Those are very good questions. Why would someone go to the trouble of stealing Violet's turkey sign and then show up at the movie with it?"

"It could be just a prank," Violet said.

"I think someone planned the whole thing," Henry said. "The turkey thief knew where the door was so that he or she could make a quick escape. Also, there was the chair that was jammed against the door."

"Do you think something will happen at

the football game tomorrow?" Benny asked, yawning.

"I don't know," Jessie said. "But we will be on the lookout."

The next morning, the children ate a quick breakfast. Henry read them the story from the newspaper. There was a picture of Mr. Tipton's office with all the boxes and cans spilled on the floor. The story told about the stolen donation jar. And it continued the story of the mystery of the missing turkey sign. At the end of the story, the reporter asked, "Where will the giant turkey show up next?"

When they arrived at the high school, the children had a plan. There was only one gate for fans to come into the stadium. The children would stand at the gate and watch all the donation bins. When they got full, Henry and Violet would take the bins back to a storage spot right behind the football players' bench. Coach Stanton had lent them some pushcarts to use. The players and the fans could see the donated goods. Nobody could steal them without being seen.

Henry was right. It was a very crowded game. It seemed as if all of Greenfield had come to watch the football team win the division championship. Even Grandfather and Mrs. McGregor had come to the game. Mr. Carroll from the hardware store, Colette from the office supply store, and Mr. Tipton were at the game. Ms. Sweeney, the reporter from the *Greenfield Times*, came and brought a photographer with her, as well. She asked the children if there was any sign of Tom the turkey. She said her readers were following the story closely. She said a lot of people were buying the newspaper to find out what had happened to the turkey.

Henry and Violet were very busy pushing the carts back and forth between the gate and the players' bench. Jessie and Benny collected the donations and gave out the tickets.

Jessie was surprised to see Ms. Matthews. She carried a bag full of canned goods. She placed it in the bin.

"Thank you for the donation," Jessie said.

Ms. Matthews smiled at her. "I'm still hoping that I am wrong," she said. Ten minutes later, Mr. Higgins came to the gate. He also had a very large bag full of donated goods.

"Thank you, Mr. Higgins!" Jessie said. "You are very generous."

"I am happy to help." Mr. Higgins looked down at the donation bins. Jessie noticed that most of the bags in the bins were from Higgins's Grocery Store. Mr. Higgins noticed it too. He smiled.

After all the tickets were sold, Henry, Jessie, Violet, and Benny were invited to sit with the players on the sidelines. They could watch the game and also keep an eye on the large pile of donations behind them. Mr. Grayson paced back and forth behind the bench. He was very happy about the large amount of donations. But Jessie thought that he seemed nervous as well.

Benny was very excited. "Look at me!" he cried. "I'm a football player!" One of the players had put a helmet on Benny's head.

Henry tossed a ball to Benny. "Good catch, Benny!" Henry said.

"Do you think I can try running on the field at halftime?" Benny asked. "I want to be a football player!"

"I'm not sure," Henry said. "You might not be allowed. Usually the band plays at halftime."

"The band?" asked Benny.

Henry pointed to the section in the stands where the band members were sitting in their bright red uniforms, holding their instruments.

"Wow! That will be cool," Benny said. "When is halftime?"

Jessie looked at the scoreboard. "Halftime is in just a few minutes," she said.

Soon, the referee blew his whistle. The Greenfield team was winning by three points. The players all ran to the locker room. Then the band marched out onto the field. Everyone lined up and held their instruments. But before they started to play, Mr. Grayson walked out onto the field. He had a microphone. He thanked everyone for their donations. He told them that the food pantry was almost ready to open. The crowd clapped loudly. Mr. Grayson also announced that Green Fields restaurant would give a free turkey dinner on Thanksgiving to anyone who needed it.

Then the music started. There were flags and horns and banging drums. There were girls who wore capes and twirled batons. Benny clapped his hands. The music was loud. He felt like the drums were banging in his stomach! He wished he could march in the band, too.

Suddenly, the crowd started to mumble. Something was happening. The children could not see. Some people began to laugh and point.

"Look!" Violet cried. "There is something that is trying to march with the band! What is it?"

"I see it! It's Tom the turkey!" Benny cried. "Stop!" Benny raced onto the field and soon disappeared into the marching band.

"Benny! Wait!" Jessie cried.

Henry, Jessie, and Violet ran after their little brother. They tried to be careful. They did not want to bump into anyone from the band. The band members looked very surprised. They tried to keep playing and marching. The crowd was laughing harder. Everyone could see the tall head of the turkey. It was moving quickly across the field. Henry, Jessie, and Violet tried to follow the turkey as quickly as they could. Finally, they got through the band. They looked all around. But they did not see the turkey. They only saw Benny. He was running into the end zone. He was still wearing the big helmet. He looked like a very small football player.

When Henry, Jessie, and Violet caught up with Benny, they were all out of breath.

"I couldn't catch him," Benny said. "He ran through there." Benny pointed to an opening in the fence.

Someone dressed in black jumped into a big car that was parked on the other side of the fence behind some bushes. The children could just see Tom the turkey's feet sticking out of the trunk. The car raced away.

"You almost got him, Benny," Henry said.

"I really want him back!" Benny said. "He should be outside of the food pantry. Violet made him! He would let everyone know where the food pantry is. Why won't they give him back?"

The second half of the game was very exciting. The Greenfield football team won. Everyone cheered. But Benny sat on the sidelines. His head was in his hands.

Coach Stanton stopped next to Benny. "This is for you," he said. He handed Benny a football. "You ran very fast into the end zone. You almost caught that big turkey. When you are old enough to go to high school, I want you to be a player on our team."

"Really?" Benny said.

"Yes," said Coach Stanton. "You are very fast. And I am sure you will be a good football player." All the football players clapped for Benny.

Grandfather and Mrs. McGregor were

there, as well. "I am proud of all of you children," Grandfather said. "Look at how many donations you have collected."

"It's enough to feed the whole town!" Mrs. McGregor said.

"It is a lot," Henry said. "We will need some help to get everything to the food pantry."

"Where is Mr. Grayson?" asked Jessie.

"I haven't seen him since halftime," Grandfather said. "I'm sure he must be around here somewhere. We can put some of the donations in my car."

"I'll help, too." Mr. Carroll from the hardware store was there as well. "I have a truck and I can fit many of the bags."

The children loaded the food onto the carts and pushed them into the parking lot. They helped place all the bags into Grandfather's trunk and into Mr. Carroll's truck.

"It won't all fit!" Benny said.

Just then, Mr. Grayson drove into the parking lot. "Hello!" he called. He pulled up next to the Aldens. "Sorry to be late. I had an emergency at the restaurant. I think we can fit the rest of these bags into my trunk."

The children carried the last bags to Mr. Grayson's car. As Jessie placed her bag in the trunk, she saw something. She quietly picked it up and put it in her pocket.

When the cars were loaded, everyone drove to the food pantry. Mr. Grayson unlocked the door and everyone unloaded the packages.

"What a bright and cheerful place!" Mrs. McGregor cried.

"Thanks to the Aldens," Mr. Grayson said. "They cleaned up and painted the walls."

"When do you think the food pantry will be able to open?" asked Grandfather.

"I was hoping to open it on Friday," Mr. Grayson said. "But since tomorrow is Thanksgiving, and I will be cooking for everyone at the restaurant, I won't have time to set it up. Maybe next week."

"We can help," Violet said. "We can put everything on the shelves tomorrow morning."

"And then we could come to the restaurant

and help with serving the meals to the needy," Jessie said.

"That would be fantastic!" Mr. Grayson said.

Benny left a small bowl of cat food in the alley for Sunny. She was shy with all the people around and had hidden from them.

Henry, Jessie, Violet, and Benny climbed into Grandfather's car. "Are you children sure that you do not mind having Thanksgiving at the restaurant? It will be hard work. You will be serving people and cleaning up plates. You will not be able to relax at home on the holiday."

"We're sure, Grandfather," Jessie said. "Mrs. McGregor makes wonderful meals for us every night. We want to make sure that people who don't have as much as we do can have a good Thanksgiving meal."

Just then there was a loud growl in the car. Even Grandfather was startled.

Benny's face turned red. "My stomach can't help it!" he cried. "Everyone keeps talking about food!"

"I have a nice warm stew in the slow-cooker," Mrs. McGregor said. "And I baked a fresh loaf of wheat bread this morning. We can eat as soon as we get home."

Jessie was the only one not thinking about food. She kept her hand in her pocket. She was holding something, and she wanted to show it to her sister and brothers.

CHAPTER 10

Two Confessions

Benny dipped a thick slice of fresh bread into his stew. He was still holding the football that the coach had given to him after the game.

"Benny," Grandfather said. "Why don't you go put your football in your room?"

"I need to carry the football everywhere, Grandfather," Benny said. "I have to practice so I can be on the team when I am in high school."

"I thought you liked the band," Violet said.

"I did!" Benny scooped a potato chunk into his mouth. "I liked both. I am going to play football, and then I will play in the band at halftime. I want to play the drums."

Everyone talked about how much fun the football game had been. It was exciting that Greenfield High had won the championship. After dinner, the children helped Mrs. McGregor in the kitchen. She was baking pumpkin pies to donate for the free Thanksgiving dinner at Green Fields restaurant. Soon, the whole table was filled with delicious pies.

"We'll let them cool," Mrs. McGregor said. "I will put them in boxes later. All except for this one."

"Is there something wrong with that one?" asked Benny.

Mrs. McGregor shook her head. "No, but I made one pie too many. Do you have any ideas what we could do with it?"

"Eat it!" Benny cried. "Did you make that pie for us?"

Mrs. McGregor cut four large slices of pie.

"I sure did," she said.

Jessie poured glasses of cold milk. The children sat in the warm kitchen to eat the pumpkin pie.

"We will have to leave early tomorrow morning," Jessie said. "It will take a long time to empty all those bags and put all the food on the shelves."

"Grandfather will drop us off at the food pantry," Henry said. "He is going into town to take Mrs. McGregor's pies to Green Fields restaurant."

Violet poured herself another glass of milk. "Did you know that Grandfather and Mr. Carroll and Colette have offered to drive people to the Thanksgiving dinner?"

Benny licked a dab of whipped cream from his fork. "But why don't they drive themselves?" he asked.

"Some are not healthy enough to drive," Henry said. "And some people don't have cars."

"Grandfather said that some of our neighbors have already volunteered to drive others to the food pantry once it opens," Jessie said.

"There are a lot of thoughtful people in Greenfield," Violet said. "But I hope they can find the food pantry. I wish it was not in such a hidden spot."

Suddenly, Jessie remembered what she had in her pocket. She pulled it out and set it on the table.

"What's that?" asked Benny.

"I found it in the trunk of Mr. Grayson's car today," Jessie said.

Henry and Violet looked surprised. It was a curled piece of twine. It looked very much like the twine Mr. Carroll had used to tie down Violet's turkey sign.

"We will need to work fast at the food pantry tomorrow," Jessie said. "Because when we are done, I think I know where we can find Violet's giant turkey sign."

"You know where Tom the turkey is?" Benny asked. He was so excited that he dropped his football, and it rolled across the floor.

"Maybe," Jessie said. "But we will know for sure tomorrow."

The next morning, Mrs. McGregor made an especially big Thanksgiving Day breakfast. The children ate platefuls of eggs and bacon and French toast.

"Thank you, Mrs. McGregor!" Violet said. "That was delicious."

Mrs. McGregor smiled. "I'm glad you liked it. You children have a very big Thanksgiving Day ahead with all of your volunteering. I wanted you to have a good start to the day."

After breakfast, Grandfather drove the children to the food pantry. Henry used the key to open the door. Everyone was glad that no one had played any tricks. There was no trash thrown on the door. The sign that Violet had painted on the door still looked very nice.

The children worked quickly. Benny was in charge of lining up the cereal boxes. Henry stacked the heavy cans of soup and sauce. Jessie set all the vegetables side-by-side. Violet made signs to place on the shelves so that everyone would be able to find what they were looking for.

Soon, the food pantry looked just like a regular store. All the cans and boxes were neatly on the shelves. The floor was swept clean and the lights shone brightly. Violet's signs explained where all the food could be found.

The children were just about ready to leave when they heard a banging on the door.

"Oh no!" Violet said. "Do you think the person who played all the tricks is back?"

Henry carefully opened the door. "It's Mr. Higgins!" he said.

Mr. Higgins walked into the food pantry. He was wearing a dark brown hat and scarf. He looked around at all the food stacked on the shelves. "It looks very nice in here," he said. "I think that you children have done a wonderful job. I have to admit that I am very embarrassed. In the beginning, I hated the food pantry. I was worried. I thought that no one would shop at my grocery store. I thought everyone would come for the free food at the food pantry."

"We're sorry," Jessie said. "We did not want the food pantry to hurt your grocery store."

"But it didn't!" Mr. Higgins said. "It helped my grocery store! When you had the food pantry movie night and football game, my store was very crowded. Everyone in Greenfield wanted to buy cans of beans and vegetables and boxes of cereal to donate to the food pantry. My business has never been better."

"That's wonderful," Jessie said.

"It made me realize something," Mr. Higgins said. "I was being selfish. I was not thinking. People who shop at my store will not go to the food pantry. They will buy groceries at my store to donate to the food pantry. And people who are hungry will now have a place to go to find something to eat."

"We are glad that you stopped by to tell us," Violet said.

Mr. Higgins pulled out his wallet. "I came to confess," he said, "and to pay you back for what I have done. I am ashamed to tell you that I am the one who threw garbage on the door, put holes in your bicycle tires, and broke the glass jars in your baskets. I even ripped your fliers off the store windows."

Violet looked at Mr. Higgins' brown hat and scarf. "You were the man who knocked into Mr. Grayson in the street and spilled all the canned goods."

"Yes. I'm sorry," Mr. Higgins said.

Benny jumped up and down. "What about Tom the turkey? Did you steal the sign? Can you give it back now?"

Mr. Higgins looked surprised. "Yes, Benny. I did take it. I was very angry. I took the sign at night after you went home. I threw it in the alley behind my store, and now it is gone. I want to give you some money so that you can make a new sign. I am very sorry for what I have done."

Jessie shook her head. "We think we know where the sign is," she said. "We are on our way there now."

Henry locked the door and everyone

headed down Chestnut Street. When they were still a block away, they saw something strange. Ms. Sweeney, the reporter, was outside taking pictures. Tom the turkey was sitting on the roof of Green Fields restaurant!

"What is he doing up there?" Benny asked excitedly.

The children and Mr. Higgins rushed inside the restaurant. Mr. Grayson and Ms. Matthews were sitting at a table, but for once they were not fighting. Grandfather was there, as well.

Violet noticed that the chairs had green leaves painted on the sides. She remembered that the chair she had seen outside the theater had the same design.

Benny ran up to Mr. Grayson. "Tom the turkey is on your roof!" he cried.

"Mr. Grayson already knows that," Jessie said. "Because he was the one who put Tom the turkey on the roof."

Mr. Grayson's face turned red. "You are right, Jessie."

"But why would you steal the turkey?"

Benny asked. "He was supposed to show everyone where the food pantry was. We have been trying to find him for days!"

"I know. I'm sorry, Benny. I did not mean to upset you. I did not steal the turkey sign first. Someone else did. But I found it in the alley behind Mr. Higgins's grocery store. I wrapped it up in plastic and snuck it to my house. Ms. Matthews saw me carrying the package."

"I was very suspicious," Ms. Matthews said. "But I did not know that it was the turkey sign. You hid it very well in that plastic wrapping."

"You should have given it back," Benny said.

"I should have, Benny. But I will tell you why I did not. I kept it to help the food pantry. I wanted everyone to know that Greenfield had a food pantry. I called the newspaper to tell them about the missing turkey sign. The next day, the news about the food pantry was on the front page! I wanted more stories about the food pantry. If the turkey stayed missing, there would be more news stories."

"You snuck into the theater, too." Jessie said. "You are the one who ran with the turkey across the movie screen and across the football field."

"I did," Mr. Grayson said. "The first day, I needed to check to make sure that there was a door in the theater that I could use to escape without being seen. I had to run fast because Benny saw me from the small window in the projection room."

Violet pointed to the chair that Mr. Grayson was sitting in. "You used one of the chairs from your restaurant to hold the door shut. That is why we could not catch you the night of the movie."

"I almost did not get the door shut in time," Mr. Grayson said. "It's a good thing I had help."

Noreen had brought in a tray of sandwiches and drinks. "Sorry, kids," she said. "But it was all for a good cause."

"It *was* for a good cause," Mr. Grayson said. "Because now everyone in Greenfield knows that Violet's beautiful turkey sign is for the food pantry. When we put it back outside the alley, no one will ever have trouble finding the food pantry again."

"You sure can run fast with Tom the turkey," Benny said. "I could not catch you. But at least I got to run on the football field."

Mr. Grayson turned to Grandfather. "Your grandchildren are not only helpful, they are very good at solving mysteries, as well."

"What happened to the money that was stolen from Mr. Tipton's office at the movie theater?" asked Henry.

"It wasn't *really* stolen," Mr. Grayson said. "I still have it. I am going to use it tomorrow to buy fresh fruit and vegetables for the food pantry from Mr. Higgins's grocery store. I am sorry about making a mess in Mr. Tipton's office. I thought it would make the newspaper story more interesting. "

"I would like to help," Mr. Higgins said. "I know many things about how to run a store. I would be proud to be a part of the food pantry. And I feel very bad about some of the things I have done." Mr. Higgins told

Mr. Grayson what he had confessed to the children. "I want to make it up to you."

"That would be wonderful," Mr. Grayson said. "Thank you."

Ms. Matthews stood up. "I need to get back to my restaurant," she said. "There is a lot of work to do. A lot of people have made reservations for Thanksgiving dinner tonight. But I will be back to help here when I am done. I also want to do my part to help the needy."

"So you are not angry about the food pantry anymore?" asked Jessie.

Ms. Matthews smiled. "No. But I was right about Mr. Grayson. He certainly is sneaky. I think he should have let us know what he was doing. We all could have helped him. And I would not have been so suspicious. But it was for a good cause. So I am not angry. I know now that he is a good man. I hope we will be neighbors for a long time. Green Fields is giving a free Thanksgiving dinner to the needy tonight. But Harvest Restaurant will also be full of customers. There is room enough for two good restaurants in Greenfield."

Later that night after all the food was cooked, Henry, Jessie, Violet, and Benny helped to serve all the people who had come to Green Fields restaurant for the free Thanksgiving meal. It was hard work, but they were glad to do it. They were thankful that they lived with Grandfather, that Mrs. McGregor cooked good meals for them every day, and that they had made wonderful friends in Greenfield. They were happy that so many hungry people had a good Thanksgiving meal at the restaurant.

After all the dishes had been cleaned up and all the guests went home, Henry, Jessie, Violet, Benny, Grandfather, Mr. Grayson, Noreen, and Ms. Matthews sat down to eat their Thanksgiving meal. The food was delicious. Afterward, they ate more of Mrs. McGregor's pumpkin pie.

"I can't eat another bite," said Mr. Grayson. "I am stuffed."

"Me, too," said Ms. Matthews.

Benny finished up his second piece of pie.

"Listen, everyone!" he said.

The table became very quiet. Everyone listened.

"I don't hear anything," Grandfather finally said.

"Neither do I," said Henry.

"I know!" cried Benny. "I don't hear anything either. My stomach has finally stopped growling!"

Everyone laughed.

"It is a good feeling to know that no one in Greenfield will have to have a growling stomach tonight," Ms. Matthews said. She raised her glass to toast Mr. Grayson.

"Thank you," Mr. Grayson said. "But I could never have done it without the Aldens."

Henry, Jessie, Violet, and Benny were very tired. Their arms ached from all the platters of food they had carried out of the kitchen all night long. But they had helped to feed many hungry people. They raised their glasses of apple cider.

"To our best Thanksgiving ever," Henry said.

Jessie, Violet, and Benny smiled and clinked their glasses with Henry's. "To our best Thanksgiving ever!"